The holiday season is a time when we remember with warmth and appreciation friends who mean the most to us; a time when we realize how important it is to be *in the company of friends.* Your Tupperware family wants you to know how much we appreciate your friendship — how important you are to us — and wish you health, happiness and continued success in the coming year.

Your friends at THP

A Friend Is Special

Your friendship is a treasured part
Of all the riches in my heart;
Your friendliness will quiet fears
That may arise through coming years;
Your friendship sings a golden song
And keeps my spirits high and strong.
I shall be grateful all my days
Because you walked in friendship ways.

Roy Z. Kemp

ISBN 0-89542-051-1

Friendship Garden

I have a friendship garden,
    Of flowers, and shrubs and trees,
A dear old-fashioned garden,
    With butterflies and bees:
Each flower's a glowing memory
    Of friends, both far and near,
Who shared their gardens with me
    To make my garden here;

For lilacs, white and purple,
    And roses, sweet and fair,
And violets and myrtle
    All blossom sweetly there.
Each flower is a token
    Of friends I love so well,
A message mutely spoken
    That only flowers tell.

To wander in this garden,
    When dusk comes stealing through,
This sweet, old-fashioned garden,
    Bedecked with sparkling dew,
Brings back to me the faces
    Of friends whom I hold dear;
They tread with me the mazes,
    I feel their presence near.

Dora P. Fortner

Found— a New World

When you've found someone most perfect,
Someone that's more than a friend,
Someone that makes your life different,
Someone you'd trust to the end,

You're living in a new world, all your own,
A world full of all things nice,
A world that no one could purchase
For gold or any price.

You, then, have something to live for,
Something to look forward to,
Something that makes you feel
That you're glad you're really you.

Gertrude Williams Siesholtz

The essence of friendship is entireness,
a total magnanimity and trust.

Ralph Waldo Emerson

Friendship Means

Listening to heartaches and cares,
Happiness that another one shares,
Whispering a kind word or two,
Sunshine when storm clouds are due,
Comfort when all else goes wrong,
Laughter, a smile and a song.

Esther Lloyd Dauber

Familiar Sounds

So many sounds are sweet to hear
That daily fall on listening ear:
The whisper of a summer breeze
As it blows softly through the trees,
The silver raindrops' rhythmic beat
That dance upon our village street.

Familiar sounds I like to hear
That daily tell me God is near:
A peal of laughter from a child,
An ocean's roar, so loud and wild,
The stir of spring when winter ends,
The happy greetings of true friends.

These cheerful sounds are sweet to hear
Whene'er they fall upon my ear.

Carice Williams

A loving friendship does not age,
It doesn't have the time;
For thought and care and helpfulness
Are always in their prime.

Craig E. Sathoff

Lifelong Friends

Lifelong friends, what lovelier thing
    Could the hand of life bestow
Than a friendship built upon
    All the precious things you know:
Faith in each other and the ties
    Of understanding old and wise.

A friendship flavored by the past,
    Old swimmin' holes and days shot through
With loafin', fishin', catchin' crabs,
    The crazy things that small boys do,
A hideout in the woods somewhere,
    Adventure on the bill-of-fare.

School days and hockey, bikes and skates,
    A girl's face tangled in your heart,
Your first small job that in some way
    Became the groundwork of your start,
The glamour of a high school dance
    That seemed all beauty and romance.

These are the ties, the little things
    That add up to the kindly sum
Of all that makes the days worthwhile,
    The precious memories that become
As strong as a hempen rope to bear
    The strands of friendship woven there.

Earth holds no greater good I think
Than friendship welded link by link.

Edna Jaques

Friends

Friends are like the sturdy oaks that rustle in the breeze when the summer suns are gone . . . Like the boughs of spicy evergreens pressed against our lives to shelter from the wintry blast . . . Friends are like low blooming flowers that break at spring to light our path . . . Like the perfumed roses dropping petals of happiness around our door . . . Friends are like green mosses clinging close to running brooks . . . Like the flowing streams spreading their moisture along the fields and asking no reward or pay . . . Friends are like the shady nooks giving sweet release at evening's hush . . . Like the broad expanse of softest green and copper bronze to delight the eye . . . Friends are like the gentle whisperings of a love divine . . . Forgiving and forgetting without a tinge of blame.

Betha Keiningham

Your Friendship

Your friendship is the glowing sun . . . That warms the winding road . . . And lightens every step I take . . . Beneath my daily load . . . It is the soft and silvery note . . . That leaves the convent bell . . . The tender flower that I pick . . . To wear in my lapel . . . It is the murmur of the brook . . . The laughter of a child . . . And all the fragrance and romance . . . Of woods and grasses wild . . . Your friendship is the echo in . . . The hills that hold the dawn . . . And every dream that lingers when . . . The purple dusk is gone . . . It is the quiet gentleness . . . Of winds that walk the sea . . . It is the all-embracing gift . . . My God has given me.

James J. Metcalfe

The joy of this world, when you have summed it up,
is found in the making of friends.

William C. Wolfmuller

Pebbles

Drop a pebble in the water,
    Watch the ripples run,
See them as they flash and glimmer
    In the noonday sun.

        Then remember acts of kindness
            Are like pebbles, too.
        Dropped into the water they send
            Many ripples, too.

You don't know just how outreaching
    Acts of kindness are,
But they ripple gently shoreward;
    What blessings they are!

        Just a simple act of kindness
            Ripples to the shore
        Echoing, reechoing,
            And what's even more,

Think of all the friends you'll gather!
    Pebbles, one by one,
Dropped into the still, still waters
    Make the ripples run.

                        Georgia B. Adams

The collected pleasures of everyday life fade
away quickly unless there is at the heart of
them the gladness of having done something
that has made someone happier.

Author Unknown

If you have but a solitary friend, who is tried and true, you are among the rich in mind and heart. You then have an investment that never loses its value. You will grow richer each day of your life. Once you have that kind of friendship, do not expect too much of it. Measure it out. Give to it all the loyalty that is yours, and what a possession you will then have!

George Matthew Adams

Our Friendship's Like a Garden

Our friendship's like a garden,
Filled with kind and loving things,
Like sunny smiles and outstretched hands
And butterflies with wings.

Our friendship's like a garden,
Filled with blessings sweet and true,
The kind that come from up above
And give real joy to you.

Patricia Emme

Best of all is it to preserve everything in a pure,
still heart, and let there be for every pulse a
thanksgiving, and for every breath a song.

Gesner

Friendship

Friendship is the thread of gold
    In the Master Weaver's design
Which, woven into life's fabric,
    Gives it extra sparkle and shine.

This thread which holds our hearts together
    Gets stronger with each passing year
As each realizes its worth
    And learns to hold friends more dear.

I cannot trace the many threads,
    But I know the design is true,
It has been proven by several years
    Of having a friend like you.

Hazel Ramsay White

Cherished Possessions

A friend who is tried and proven true,
    A companion who's interested in all I do,

A child that snuggles close to my heart,
    A loved one who is of my life a treasured part,

A garden with blossoms rare,
    The scent of roses permeating the air,

The ability to ever smile,
    For little things that make life worthwhile,

Memories that passing time endears,
    And links together the happy years,

For daydreams that bring you ever near,
    While I'm wishing you were really here,

For sunrays that drive out the gloom,
    For beautiful pictures from life's loom,

New friends that I have made this year,
    Old friends who have grown more dear.

Wauneta Hackleman

Friends

Among the blessings which God sends
To enrich our lives throughout the years,
Is the gracious love of faithful friends
Who share with us our hopes and fears.

They match the beauty of the flowers
And thoughts of them are very sweet;
Their memory brightens lonely hours
As time slips by on hurried feet.

'Tis good to feel, as time goes on
Relentless in it's speedy flight,
That we have love and friendship won
Of those who cherish what is right.

John Everington

The House by the Side of the Road

There are hermit souls that live withdrawn
  In the peace of their self-content;
There are souls, like stars, that dwell apart
  In a fellowless firmament;
There are pioneer souls that blaze their paths
  Where highways never ran;
But let me live by the side of the road
  And be a friend to man.

Let me live in a house by the side of the road,
  Where the race of men go by —
The men who are good and the men who are bad,
  As good and as bad as I;
I would not sit in the scorner's seat,
  Or hurl the cynic's ban;
Let me live in a house by the side of the road
  And be a friend to man.

I see from my house by the side of the road,
  By the side of the highway of life,
The men who press with the ardor of hope,
  The men who are faint with the strife.
But I turn not away from their smiles nor their tears —
  Both parts of an infinite plan;
Let me live in my house by the side of the road
  And be a friend to man.

I know there are brook-gladdened meadows ahead,
  And mountains of wearisome height,
That the road passes on through the long afternoon
  And stretches away to the night.
But still I rejoice when the travelers rejoice
  And weep with the strangers that moan,
Nor live in my house by the side of the road
  Like a man who dwells alone.

Let me live in my house by the side of the road
  Where the race of men go by —
They are good, they are bad, they are weak, they are strong,
  Wise, foolish — so am I.
Then why should I sit in the scorner's seat
  Or hurl the cynic's ban?
Let me live in my house by the side of road
  And be a friend to man.

Sam Walter Foss

I Stand
on the Shore

I stand on the shore, throwing pebbles into the lake;
It amuses the children to see the waves they make.
And I laugh their laughter as my child sings
Songs of acceptance their friendship brings.
    How short the day's warmth,
    How quick the cold from the ground.

          It's time to go home; they ask me to stay,
          But a distant voice calls me to a place far away.
             Roads cross and recross,
             Crisscrossing in time.
          Another day, another me, will meet another you
          And then, my friend, we'll talk as strangers
          Remembering how we grew.

Jerry Whelan

If I Can Stop
One Heart
from Breaking

If I can stop one heart from breaking,
I shall not live in vain;
If I can ease one life the aching,
Or cool one pain,
Or help one fainting robin
Unto his nest again,
I shall not live in vain.

Emily Dickinson

A Lovely Light

A candle's but a simple thing,
    It starts with just a bit of string;
Yet dipped and dipped with patient hand,
    It gathers wax upon the strand
Until, complete and snowy white,
    It gives at last a lovely light.

Life seems so like that bit of string,
    Each deed we do a simple thing;
Yet day by day if on life's strand,
    We work with patient heart and hand;
It gathers joy, makes dark days bright,
    And gives at last a lovely light.

Clara Bell Thurston

Friendship

Oh, the comfort, the inexpressible
  comfort, of feeling safe with a person,
Having neither to weigh thoughts
Nor measure words, but pouring them
All right out just as they are,
Chaff and grain together,
Certain that a faithful hand will
Take and sift them,
Keep what is worth keeping
And with the breath of kindness
Blow the rest away.

Dinah Maria Mulock Craik

While Such Friends Are Near Us

Those are red-letter days in our lives when we meet people who thrill us like a fine poem, people whose handshakes are brimful of unspoken sympathy and whose sweet, rich natures impart to our eager, impatient spirits a wonderful restlessness which, in its essence, is divine.

The perplexities, irritations and worries that have absorbed us pass like unpleasant dreams, and we wake to see with new eyes and hear with new ears the beauty and harmony of God's real world. The solemn nothings that fill our everyday life blossom suddenly into bright possibilities.

In a word, while such friends are near us we feel that all is well. Perhaps we never saw them before and they may never cross our life's path again; but the influence of their calm, mellow natures is a libation poured upon our discontent, and we feel its healing touch as the ocean feels the mountain stream freshening its brine.

Helen Keller

Lovely Garden

Make the heart a lovely garden,
Ever cautious what you sow;
Fill each space with deeds of kindness
Where the seeds of friendship grow.

Lace each path with bright thought-flowers,
Let their fragrance waft so sweet,
Unkind words, like weeds and shadows,
Feel unwelcome and retreat.

June Masters Bacher

Friendship

You have to work at friendship
　　Like a gardener with his flowers,
Cherish the tiny buds of love,
　　Treasure the happy hours,

Plant loving seeds for future bloom,
　　Pluck out the weeds and tares,
Water the soil with loving deeds,
　　And firm it down with prayers.

You have to work at friendship,
　　With a tenderness and zeal,
Drawing your friends into your heart,
　　With roots as strong as steel,
Shaping the growth with loving thought
　　As careful gardeners do,
If love and peace and happiness
　　Will ever bloom for you.

For friendship is a tender plant
　　Of bud and root and vine,
Frail as the mist above the hills,
　　Fragrant as myrrh and pine,
Rooted in earth, its branches reach
　　Beyond the farthest sea,
Yet clings in little tender words
　　Between my friend and me.

And like all worthwhile things it pays
Dividends in a hundred ways.

Edna Jaques

Two Smiles

I smiled at a child this morning,
    And the smile that came back to me
Was so sweet and as refreshing
    As ever a smile could be.

    To me it was such a blessing
        Her dear little face to see,
    When I smiled at a child this morning
        And she smiled back at me.

Her sweet smiling face at the window
    In my memory long I'll see;
Since I smiled at a child in passing,
    And her smile came to me.

    Only two smiles flashed between us
        In a fleeting instant of time,
    Yet mine carried gladness to her heart
        And hers beamed a blessing to mine.

Lorena B. Galloway

The Arrow and the Song

I shot an arrow into the air,
It fell to earth, I knew not where;
For, so swiftly it flew, the sight
Could not follow it in its flight.

I breathed a song into the air,
It fell to earth, I knew not where;
For who has sight so keen and strong
That can follow the flight of song?

Long, long afterward in an oak,
I found the arrow, still unbroke;
And the song, from beginning to end,
I found again in the heart of a friend.

Henry Wadsworth Longfellow

Friendship is the simple reflections
of souls by each other.

William Alger

It is a beautiful necessity of our nature
to love something.

Jerrold

The happiest moments of my life
have been in the flow of affection among friends.

Thomas Jefferson

Blessed are they who have the gift of making friends, for it is one of God's best gifts. It involves many things, but above all, the power of going out of oneself, and appreciating whatever is noble and loving in another.

Thomas Hughes

Friendship Basket

I know someone who visits friends,
A basket at her side,
Replete with portions of her heart
And joy her hands provide.

She'll bring a freshly minted tea,
Perhaps a book or two,
The jam she made one summer day,
A daffodil she grew.

For giving is a happiness
That spreads from just a start
By someone with a basketful
Of treasures from the heart.

Virginia Covey Boswell

If, instead of a gem or even a flower, we could cast the gift of a lovely thought into the heart of a friend, that would be giving as the angels give.

George McDonald

The Friend
Who Just Stands By

When trouble comes your soul to try,
You love the friend who just "stands by."
Perhaps there's nothing he can do—
The thing is strictly up to you;
For there are troubles all your own,
And paths the soul must tread alone;
Times when love cannot smooth the road
Nor friendship lift the heavy load,
But just to know you have a friend
Who will "stand by" until the end,
Whose sympathy through all endures,
Whose warm handclasp is always yours—
It helps, someway, to pull you through,
Although there's nothing he can do.
And so with fervent heart you cry,
"God bless the friend who just 'stands by'!"

B. Y. Williams

Friendship Is

Friendship is a tender thing,
It's every joy that life can bring:
A bit of hope, a heart so true,
So much another shares with you;
It's courage when life brings a frown,
To lend a hand when you are down.

Friendship is believing still
Whene'er the road seems all uphill,
Encouragement, a word of praise
To brighten up those darker days,
Companionship and loving trust,
True friendship is a sacred must.

Friendship is a two-way street
Where smiles are bright and dear ones meet;
It's reaching out in time of need
And helping with a kindly deed;
It's taking time to share a smile,
Just being thoughtful all the while.

It's loyalty and peace serene,
Remembering to share your dream,
A comforter when things go wrong,
A guiding light amid the throng,
A faith, a hope, a bright new day.
Friendship is a chosen way.

Garnett Ann Schultz

Life is to be fortified by many friendships.
To love and to be loved is the greatest happiness
of existence.

Sydney Smith

Richer Today

You are richer today than you were yesterday . . . if you have laughed often, given something, forgiven even more, made a new friend today, or made stepping-stones of stumbling-blocks; if you have thought more in terms of "thyself" than of "myself," or if you have suc-ceeded in being cheerful even if you were weary. You are richer tonight than you were this morning . . . if you have taken time to trace the handiwork of God in the commonplace things of life, or if you have learned to count out things that really do not count, or if you have been a little blinder to the faults of friend or foe. You are richer if a little child has smiled at you, and a stray dog has licked your hand, or if you have looked for the best in others, and have given others the best in you.

Old Scrapbook

Friendship

Is a little bit of giving
And a little bit of love,
With a little bit of blessing
Coming from above.
Just a little bit of thoughtfulness
To make some pathway bright
Is all it takes for friendship
To blossom overnight.

Olive Dunkelberger

Friendship

Friendship is like a flower . . .
A joy from day to day;
But you must take good care of it
Lest it should fade away.

So always treat it gently;
And, nourished by your care,
The bud will grow and flourish
Into a blossom rare.

Cheryl June Wachsmuth

Tea Time

One of the nicest times of day,
I'm sure you will agree,
Is when you put the kettle on
At four o'clock for tea.

The little tray arranged with care,
Especially for two,
Some dainty, tasty sandwiches
And biscuits, just a few.

The bright, round teapot waiting for
The kettle's cheerful tune;
A special friend to share with you,
A happy afternoon.

A. J. Christianson

A Smile

A smile can be as lovely as a prayer,
   If there is understanding in the eyes;
A smile that says: "I'm glad to see you there,"
   A look that whispers something sweet and wise.
Old people often smile like this when they
Have special love and kindness to convey.

A baby's smile, a wee three-cornered thing,
   A bit uncertain of its right to be,
Can lift your heart clear up where angels sing
   And show you realms unguessed, eternity
Come down and held in crumpled rosy hands,
Frail in themselves yet strong as iron bands.

The smile of friendship where two eyes unite
   In friendly gossip o'er a cup of tea,
Where little happenings of the neighborhood
   Are told with relish and a kindly glee;
A lover's smile bent to his lady's face
Can make a palace of the meanest place.

The smiles between a husband and a wife
   Across a room can tell the world so much
Of living shared and love's redeeming grace,
   As intimate and tender as a touch.
A smile can be as lovely as a prayer
If there is love and understanding there.

Edna Jaques

To a friend's house
the road is never long.

Dutch Proverb

A friend is a person with whom I may be sincere. Before him I may think aloud . . . A friend may well be reckoned the masterpiece of Nature . . . I do then with my friends as I do with my books. I would have them where I can find them, but I seldom use them . . . Happy is the house that shelters a friend.

Ralph Waldo Emerson

What Is a Friend

My friend is one who smiles with me
When all the world is fair,
Yet just as surely weeps with me
When life would bring a care.
He knows my hopes and shares my fears,
Lends praise in each success,
Rejoices when my dreams come true
And never loves me less.

My friend is every happiness
And every gladness, too,
He's faithful to the very end
Though skies are gray or blue,
To lend a strength to lift my heart,
A comfort when I grieve,
It's still my friend, and he alone,
Who helps me to believe.

What is a friend? So many things:
An understanding smile,
The greatest blessing life can lend,
He's all that is worthwhile,
Through stormy days, the ups and downs,
The precious rainbow's end;
As hand in hand we walk life's road,
I thank God for my friend.

Garnett Ann Schultz

Tribute to a Friend

Were I an artist, here's what I'd do:
I'd paint a picture familiar to you.
I would sketch with grace and tactful skill
A truly dear friend whose heart did thrill
To every flower and bird and tree
As down the old lane we strolled in glee.

Then, with color of more gorgeous hue,
I would paint the hills and valleys, too,
Where we two would sit on a sunny day
Forgetting all trouble, putting cares away.

Since I'm no artist this picture remains
Locked deep in my heart where it never fades;
Like a golden mem'ry it will always be there
As a tribute my friend, to one who is dear.

Esther Johnson

The Key
to Friendship

A cup of tea on a winter day,
A walk in the new-fallen snow,
A present when least expected
Will always let her know.

The key to lasting friendship
Is to give with a loving heart,
To think of her with tenderness
Whenever you are apart.

A warm hello, a handclasp,
A talk with a neighbor, too,
A helping hand when needed
Is all that you have to do.

A friendly smile of welcome
Whenever she comes to call,
A kiss good-bye when leaving
May mean the most of all.

Most of all, understanding
Is the basic human need;
When she is troubled, just listen
And you are a good friend indeed.

Polly Perkins

Nothing can be sweeter than friendship.

Petrarch

Friends

We share these loves, my friend and I:
   Bubbling brooks, a pink and blue sky,
Delicate mists, soft winds that sing,
   Fragile snowflakes, violets in spring.
We share these loves, my friend and I:
   Ruffled curtains, a latticed pie,
Flower-filled vases, cozy nooks,
   An open fire, rows of books.
We share these loves, my friend and I:
   Happy thoughts, aims that are high,
The warmth of friendship, pleasure in giving,
   Faith in God, and real joy in living.

Adeline Roseberg

Treasured Friendship

Today I find your friendship true
As in the joyous years now past,
Causing memories of life to glow
As treasured friendships always last.

Through coming years, I know your faith
Will give me hope for each new day
And I shall walk a brighter path
Because, through love, you came my way.

May Smith White

The ornament of a house
is the friends who frequent it.

Ralph Waldo Emerson

Welcome Guest

Come, friend and guest, into my home
And sit before the fire;
It's not a palace but to me
It holds my heart's desire.
The roof may leak a bit at times
But love is always there,
As constant as the cup of tea
That is our daily fare.

The beds are clean and fresh and warm,
The food is hearty, too.
It's not the best, but what we have
We offer it to you.
So if you want to be our guest,
Just knock upon our door.
Each room will cheerfully prove to you
Love's been a guest before.

Carice Williams

Before us is a future all unknown,
   A path untrod,
Beside us a friend well loved and known—
   That friend is God.

Author Unknown

What Is a Friend?

A friend is a person of great understanding
　　Who shares all our hopes and our schemes;
A companion who listens with infinite patience
　　To all of our hopes and our dreams.

A true friend can make all our cares melt away
　　With the touch of a hand or a smile;
And with calm reassurance make everything brighter,
　　Make life always seem more worthwhile.

A friend shares so many bright moments of laughter,
　　At even the tiniest things;
What memorable hours of lighthearted gladness,
　　What pleasure the sharing can bring!

A friend is a cherished and precious possession
　　Who knows all our hopes and our fears,
Someone to treasure deep down in our heart
　　With a closeness that grows through the years.

June Sanderfoot

Understanding Folk

When I was just a little tyke,
　　And couldn't tie my shoe;
My mother gently smiled at me
　　And pulled the laces through.

Then I grew up a little bit,
　　And when beset by fears,
My Grandpa would kindly talk with me
　　Till I smiled through the tears.

How many times when I was young,
　　Some friendly soul helped me
To find a pathway through the fog,
　　An easier way to see.

God must have a special place
　　For people such as they
Who set you back upon the path
　　When you have lost your way.

Of all the people I have known,
　　The ones I highly prize
Are those who reach a helping hand,
　　The angels in disguise.

Celia M. Gordon

Friendship

There are no words to tell you
How much you mean to me;
For happy years of friendship
I'm grateful as can be.

We walk the road together
And share so many things:
The sunshine and the shadows
That time so often brings.

For your every trace of laughter
And special gaiety,
There are no words to tell you
How much you mean to me.

Hilda Butler Farr

designed by
Colleen Callahan Gonring

Editorial Director, James Kuse
Managing Editor, Ralph Luedtke
Photographic Editor, Gerald Koser
Production Editor, Stuart L. Zyduck

ACKNOWLEDGMENTS

IF YOU HAVE BUT A SOLITARY FRIEND . . . by George Matthew Adams. Used by permission of Washington Star Syndicate, Inc. IF I CAN STOP ONE HEART FROM BREAKING by Emily Dickinson. From THE COMPLETE POEMS OF EMILY DICKINSON. Edited by Thomas H. Johnson. Published by Little, Brown and Company. THE HOUSE BY THE SIDE OF THE ROAD by Sam Walter Foss. Reprinted through courtesy of Mary L. Foss. WHILE SUCH FRIENDS ARE NEAR US . . . by Helen Keller. From THE STORY OF MY LIFE by Helen Keller, 1954, Doubleday & Company, Inc. YOUR FRIENDSHIP by James J. Metcalfe. Copyrighted. Courtesy Field Enterprises, Inc. Our sincere thanks to the following author whose address we were unable to locate: John Everington for FRIENDS.